To:

_____

From:

_____

Date:

_____

Angels in the Bible ❧ Storybook ❧

by Allia Zobel Nolan

Illustrated by Alida Massari

Every visible thing in this world is put in the charge of an angel.

—St. Augustine

ZONDER**kidz**

ZONDERKIDZ

Angels in the Bible Storybook
Copyright © 2016 by Allia Zobel Nolan
Illustrations © 2016 by Alida Massari

Requests for information should be addressed to:

Zonderkidz, 3900 *Sparks Drive SE, Grand Rapids, Michigan 49546*

ISBN 978-0-310-74365-1

Editor: Barbara Herndon
Art direction & design: Mary pat Pino

Printed in China

15 16 17 18 19 20 /DHC/ 20 19 18 17 16 15 14 13 12 11 10 9 8 7 6 5 4 3 2 1

DEDICATION

For God, who in his loving kindness, created the angels to watch over, protect, and support us—without fanfare—as we navigate the joys and perils of this world; for my husband, Desmond, the closest thing to an angel I've ever known; for my mother-in-law, Angela Nolan, who recently went to her reward among the angels; for my guardian angel, thanks for always being there; for my friend, Jeanne St. John Taylor, for her loving support; and for the host of busy angels standing beside and guiding our little ones in his ways.

—Allia Zobel Nolan

DEDICATION

For all the children that are little angels in our life.

—Alida Massari

Table of Contents

From the
Old Testament

Old Testament 11

When God Turned on the Light 12

Abraham and the Three Visitors 22

Rescuing Lot 27

Tricks, Food, and Angels on the Stairway 32

Wrestling for a Blessing 39

A Talking Donkey 45

Joshua and the Commander of God's Army 52

Gideon Asks for a Sign .60

A Long-Awaited Son 66

Food for Elijah 72

King Hezekiah and One Awesome Warrior 78

Angels in the Throne Room 84

The Stranger in the Fire 89

Lion Tamer 95

Daniel's Message Gets Delayed 102

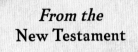

From the New Testament

New Testament 110

A Son for Zechariah. 112

A Surprise Visitor. 119

Telling Joseph about Jesus. 125

Voices Like Thunder. 130

Warning Wise Men. 138

Jesus, the Children, and the Angels. 144

Giving Strength to Jesus. 150

Delivering the Best Message Ever. 158

Watching Jesus Go Home. .166

Philip Listens and Obeys. .173

Breaking Out of Jail. 179

Jesus Is for Everybody. 186

Getting Peter Out of Prison—Again. 193

Paul Survives a Shipwreck. 201

A Better Place Filled with Angels. 210

INTRODUCTION

We've all seen cute chubby angel drawings—you know, the ones where the angel looks like your baby brother. But, actually, that's like comparing a tabby cat to a lion. An angel is anything but fluff and stuff. They are powerful, majestic beings made up of mind and spirit. What's more, they don't have bodies, except when God wants them to be seen.

Angels were created to worship and praise God. They act as his messengers and our protectors. On top of that, God sends them to announce news, guide, encourage, comfort, and answer prayers. God even sent one angel to get his friend, Peter, out of jail. Whatever way they serve God, angels always obey his will. They always give God honor and glory.

All the angels, that is, but one. This angel wanted all the praise for himself. He wanted to be better than God. So he rebelled and he and his followers wound up being thrown out of heaven. This fallen angel goes by lots of names. We know him as Satan.

But this is a book about the good angels. And there are plenty of them. How do we know they're real? Because the Bible tells us so. Yup, Scripture is filled with a bunch of stories about these awesome beings. Sometimes they are in the background, and sometimes they are the star of the story. But always, they are there, our faithful, loving friends—doing God's bidding and taking our very best interests to heart.

So what are we waiting for? Let's read about the angels.

—Allia Zobel Nolan

 Learn an *All About Angels* fact when you see this symbol.

10

OLD TESTAMENT

———◆———

The Lord will command his angels to take good care of you. They will lift you up in their hands.

Psalm 91:11–12

When God Turned on the Light

Genesis 1–2

In the beginning, God made the heavens and the earth. But they were empty, dark, and shapeless. It was very quiet, too—so quiet God could hear his own heart. It was overflowing with love.

"I'll create life," God said. "Then I can share my love." So he rolled up his sleeves and started his work. First, God got rid of the darkness with four short words. "Let there be light," he said. He called this light day, and split it from the darkness. He called that night.

"A good start," God said.

Next, God made the sky. He took it from the middle of the waters above and the waters below. He colored it blue and made it go on forever.

Then God gathered the water. He put some here, and he put some there. He called these bodies of water seas. What was left was dry ground, and God called that earth.

13

"Okay, now," God said, "let's decorate." A second later, plants, trees, and flowers sprang from the ground and turned their faces toward him.

God nodded and sweet-smelling strawberry bushes, apple and orange trees, tomato plants, tall stalks of corn, and every kind of vegetation he could imagine popped its head up and smiled.

"Carpets would be nice too," he said, and rolls of green grass spread out up and down valleys and fields. He sprinkled those with blossoms that giggled in the wind.

"We need some contrast," God said next. With that, he hung up a big, yellow fireball called sun, to mark the day. Then he made a cool, white ball he named moon to mark the night. "Let's have some sparkle," he said, and the sky lit up with twinkling stars in all shapes and sizes.

But, that wasn't all. God looked at the seas and they were empty. "We need some creatures of the deep," he said. And so he created sharks with pointy teeth, wiggly-giggly jellyfish, and manta rays. When he was finished, the waters were filled with every kind of fish he could imagine.

17

"Birds too," God said, and great eagles, skinny-legged flamingos, and swans flew, hopped, swam, and filled the earth.

Now God was happy with the fish and the birds. So he made more animals—some with long noses, like elephants and anteaters, some with stripes like tigers and zebras, animals with quills like porcupines, and long-necked giraffes. He made creepy crawly things too, like caterpillars and spiders.

"This is all really good," said God, "but …

… something is still missing. People. People who will be in my image. People who will look after what I've made. People I can share my love with."

So God made Adam and Eve, the first man and the first woman. And he poured all his love into them. God looked around one more time. He was pleased. "That's it," he said. "That's everything. And it's all very good."

Just then, thousands of angels shouted for joy. They had watched in wonder as God created everything from nothing. And when he was finished, they sang God's praises.

Imagine being there when God created the world and "… the morning stars sang together and all the angels shouted for joy." Awesome!

—Job 38:7

Abraham and the Three Visitors

Genesis 12, 18, 21

Abraham was a man of God. And he did what was right in God's eyes.

One day, God told Abraham he would have as many children as there were stars in the sky. And Abraham always trusted the Lord. It was only for a moment that he thought *Sarah and I are too old to start a family. How is this going to work?* But he chased that worry from his mind. "God always keeps his promises," he said to himself. "I'll leave the details to him."

Time passed, and one day, three strangers walked into Abraham's camp. They looked like ordinary men. But Abraham had a feeling they were angels.

"My lords," he said, "rest a while under this tree. I will see about some food and drink for you."

"As you wish," the strangers said.

So Abraham dashed off to tell Sarah three holy men were visiting. Then he asked her to prepare a meal and serve it to their guests.

After they had eaten, one of the strangers gave Abraham good news. "By this time next year," he said, "you will have a son." Abraham nearly fell over. With a message like that, he was sure it was the Lord and his angels.

In the meantime, Sarah sat in her tent. She was listening in on the conversation. When she overheard what the angel said, she laughed. *Me? Have a child at my age? How can that be?* she thought.

The Lord knew what Sarah was thinking. "Abraham," he said, loud enough for Sarah to hear, "*Some* things may not seem possible to *some* people. But believe me, everything is possible for God."

One year later, Sarah had a handsome baby boy. She called him Isaac, which means *laughing with joy.*

When angels appear, they sometimes take human bodies (probably so we can see them better).

Rescuing Lot

Genesis 19

Two of the angels who visited Abraham had another, more serious job to do. The people in the cities of Sodom and Gomorrah had turned very bad. They were wicked through and through. So the angels were on their way to deliver God's punishment. But first, they had to rescue a man named Lot.

Lot was Abraham's nephew. He and his family were once part of Abraham's camp. But the two men had so many relatives and animals and tents and workers, that there wasn't enough land for them both. So they split up. Abraham went to live in a town called Hebron. Lot and his group ended up outside Sodom and Gomorrah.

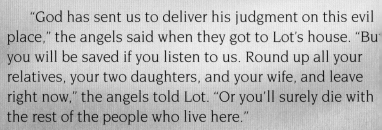

"God has sent us to deliver his judgment on this evil place," the angels said when they got to Lot's house. "But you will be saved if you listen to us. Round up all your relatives, your two daughters, and your wife, and leave right now," the angels told Lot. "Or you'll surely die with the rest of the people who live here."

Lot heard the angels. But he stood there like his feet were in cement. So the angels grabbed his hand, his daughters' hands, and his wife's hand and pulled them all out the door.

"Hurry!" the angels shouted. "We need to get out of here this minute! And whatever you do," the angels yelled, "DO NOT LOOK BACK. Keep your eyes straight ahead. Run for the mountains. DO NOT LOOK BACK!"

"The mountains?" Lot screamed. "Sirs, the mountains are too far away. We'll never make it in time. Can't we just take cover in that small town over there? Please?"

"Fine, but hurry," the angels said. "The fire will start when you're out of danger. And for the last time: DON'T LOOK BACK."

So Lot and his family started running. They ran, and they ran, and they ran.

Then, suddenly, Lot's wife slowed down. She heard the buildings crashing. She felt the heat. She smelled the smoke.

"I can't stand it anymore," she yelled at the angel. "I just have to see what's going on. God won't mind if I take one teeny tiny peek."

Lot's wife looked back over her shoulder. "Uh, oh," she said. But it was too late. In a few seconds, she turned into a statue of salt.

But Lot and the others did what they were told. They ran with their eyes straight ahead. They didn't stop. They didn't look back. And they were saved.

When everyone was settled, the angels returned to heaven. They had carried out God's orders. Their only regret was that Mrs. Lot didn't listen.

Tricks, Food, and Angels on the Stairway

Genesis 25, 27, 28

Abraham's son Isaac grew up and married a woman named Rebekah. In time, Isaac and Rebekah had twin sons. They named them Jacob and Esau. Esau was considered the firstborn. That meant he would inherit his father's wealth. It also meant he'd be the next leader of God's people … or would he?

Esau grew up to be a strong, hairy, quick-acting man. He loved hunting and eating. It didn't much matter to him that he would take his father's place someday. The future was too far away. He was more interested in what was happening now.

On the other hand, Jacob studied things more carefully. He used his mind rather than his muscles. And he loved outwitting Esau—like the day Jacob tricked Esau into handing over his first-born rights.

"I could eat a camel," Esau said when he came in from the field one day. "Whatever you're cooking, hand it over."

"It's lentil stew, Esau. And it took hours to cook," Jacob lied. "What will you give me for it? Your horse? Your birthright?"

Esau shot back without thinking. "The horse I need. Take the birthright. I can't eat *that* ... and right now, I'm starving."

Then, when their father was old and half-blind, Jacob pulled the biggest trick ever on Esau.

"I'm fading fast," Isaac said to Esau. "I must give you my blessing. But first, do your father a favor. Fix me that meat dish I like so much."

"Sure, father," Esau answered, as he left the tent.

Now just as Isaac had a soft spot in his heart for Esau, Rebekah's favorite was Jacob. So when she overheard her husband's dying request, she got an idea. *I can prepare that meal,* she thought to herself. *Jacob can dress up like Esau. Then he can bring the dish to his father. Isaac will never know the difference.* So that's what Rebekah did. Her plan worked, and Isaac gave his blessing to the wrong son. When Esau found out, there was murder in his eyes. Rebekah thought he'd kill Jacob for sure.

"Go to your uncle's and hide," she said. "Quickly."

It was nighttime when Jacob finally stopped. He hung his head and thought about the day. He was sorry he had stolen what belonged to his brother. He felt guilty he had fooled his father. And he was ashamed before God that he had lied and cheated.

All these worries wore Jacob out. So he put down a blanket, and fell asleep. When he did, he had a strange dream. It was like someone had cracked open the door to heaven and let him peek in. He knew it was heaven because he saw angels. They were doing God's work, and they looked very busy.

Suddenly, Jacob heard God speak. "I'm not happy with what you have done," God said. "But I have a plan. And you are part of it. The land you are lying on now belongs to you. That is the promise I made to your father and your grandfather. And when the time is right," God said, "I'll bring you back home."

When Jacob woke up, he was trembling. He had seen God in all his glory. He had witnessed God's angels working behind the scenes. And he had learned God had intended all along for him—not Esau—to take his father's place.

"Truly, the Lord is the one who makes things happen the way they do," Jacob said to himself. "He controls the universe. He's in charge of the angels. He makes the decisions. I realize that now."

Then Jacob took a stone and marked the spot as holy. "I name this place Bethel, or House of God," he said, "because this is where God spoke to me and showed me his angels."

Wrestling for a Blessing

Genesis 32–33: 1–4

Twenty years passed, and God told Jacob to go home. By this time, Jacob had money, a large family, servants, and lots of livestock. But he was falling back into his old bad habits. He wasn't trusting God. He was relying on himself. So God sent an angel to remind him once more just who's in charge.

"Four hundred men! Sounds like he's bringing an army," Jacob shouted when he heard Esau was on his way to meet him. "My brother is coming to kill me," he yelled. "I know it. I just know it. I better think of something … and fast."

Now what Jacob should have thought of was God's promise to protect him. And he did—for a quick second. "Lord," he prayed as he paced up and down. "You said you'd keep me safe, remember? Well, I could use your help right now."

But Jacob didn't wait and let God do his job. He was in a panic about his brother. So he came up with his own plan—just in case God had forgotten him.

"Put the animals into groups, one behind the other," Jacob said to his men. "Then walk them towards Esau. Tell him everything he has seen is his—a gift from his loving brother, Jacob. And tell him I'll meet with him tomorrow, okay?"

Now Jacob thought he was being pretty clever. He figured if he gave his brother a really big gift, Esau would not be angry any more and wouldn't try to kill him.

So nighttime came, and Jacob sent his family and flocks to follow the herders. But he stayed behind. He wanted to work out something else in case his first plan failed.

As he sat thinking, a stranger grabbed Jacob and wrestled him to the ground. Jacob fought back. The man was very strong. But Jacob held on and the two struggled all night. When the sky turned light, the man said, "Let go."

But Jacob said, "No." So the man touched Jacob's hip and broke it. That's when Jacob realized this was no stranger. This wasn't even a man. This was an angel of the Lord. And Jacob was no match for him. The angel clearly had the upper hand.

Now at first, Jacob wondered why God had sent the angel. Then, he shook his head as the reason became clear.

I'm doing it again, he thought. *I'm trying to fix things so I get my own way. And that's why this angel is here—to remind me my life is in God's hands. I can send my brother a million gifts, but God is the only one who can soften my brother's heart.*

So Jacob decided then and there to let God be in charge. But while he still had a hold of the angel, he begged him. "Please," he said, "I realize I need God's help. I can't face my brother alone. Please, give me God's blessing."

So the angel blessed him. Then he turned and looked into Jacob's eyes.

"Listen, Jacob," the angel said, "God really *does* know what he is doing—and he does everything at just the *right* time. That's a fact you have a hard time with. But I see you really want to change. So let's start with your name. Forget Jacob. You're 'Israel' from now on. It means 'struggles with God.' That ought to help you remember."

Then the angel disappeared. And it was time to meet Esau.

So Jacob limped down the path to meet his brother. He had no tricks up his sleeve. He was relying totally on God. And he didn't feel afraid.

When Esau saw Jacob, he had tears in his eyes. "Welcome home, brother," he said as he hugged Jacob. As for the angel, he was thrilled that Israel was finally trusting God completely.

A Talking Donkey

Numbers 22—24

Animals don't often get visits from angels (that we know of).
But a man called Balaam had a donkey who did. And, boy, was the
donkey surprised.

Now over the years, the Israelites (the new name for Jacob's
relatives) grew in number. Because God was with them, they
conquered all their enemies. So when a king named Balak saw the
Israelites putting up tents nearby, he was very afraid. "We need
Balaam, the seer!" he screamed. "On the double."

Now Balaam, the seer, was supposed to be able to say some words (a "curse") that could bring harm to others. So King Balak sent officials to Balaam's house to hire him.

"The king wants you to put a curse on God's people," the officals said.

"I'll sleep on it," Balaam replied. When he did, God told Balaam to refuse the king's offer. So that's what Balaam did.

A stubborn King Balak sent his officials right back with a note that read: "Come quickly and I'll triple your fee." This time, God allowed Balaam to go.

When Balaam was ready, he got on his donkey and rode off. Suddenly, she ran into a field.

"Get back on the path," Balaam yelled, and hit her. "Are you blind?"

Well, the donkey wasn't blind. She knew exactly what she was doing. She ran into the field because she saw something in the road. It was a fierce-looking angel with an even fiercer-looking sword.

A few seconds later, the angel blocked the way again. But the donkey avoided him. The third time the donkey saw the angel, she sat down rather than try to pass him. Balaam went into a rage. That's when God opened the donkey's mouth so she could speak:

"Master, can you please stop hitting me?" the donkey asked. "You know I wouldn't act this way if I didn't have a reason."

"Well, yes. You've always been a good donkey. What's the matter with you now?"

Just then, God let Balaam see the angel. When he did, he fell to the ground and bowed his head. "I wouldn't be hitting my donkey if I were you," the angel told Balaam, "especially since she saved you from my sword three times."

"Do you want me to turn around and go home?" Balaam asked.

"No," the angel replied. "God wants you to speak to his people. But when you do, say what God tells you to say—nothing else. Got that?"

So Balaam rode with the men until they arrived at the palace. Morning came and he heard God's message. Then he stood on the mountain and repeated it.

"You call that a curse?" the king bellowed when Balaam was finished.

"I can only repeat what God tells me," Balaam said.

"Try again," the king ordered. But it was no use. Balaam couldn't call evil down on the Israelites if he tried. And he tried, over and over.

"I give up," the king yelled. "You're nothing but a fake, an impostor, a fraud."

Then King Balak turned and walked away. "What did I expect?" he said to the officials. "The man talks to animals."

So Balaam gave his donkey some sweet dates and headed home. And this time, the angel got out of the donkey's way.

Can all animals see angels? We really don't know. But this time, God let the donkey see the angel before Balaam did. (Numbers 22:16–31)

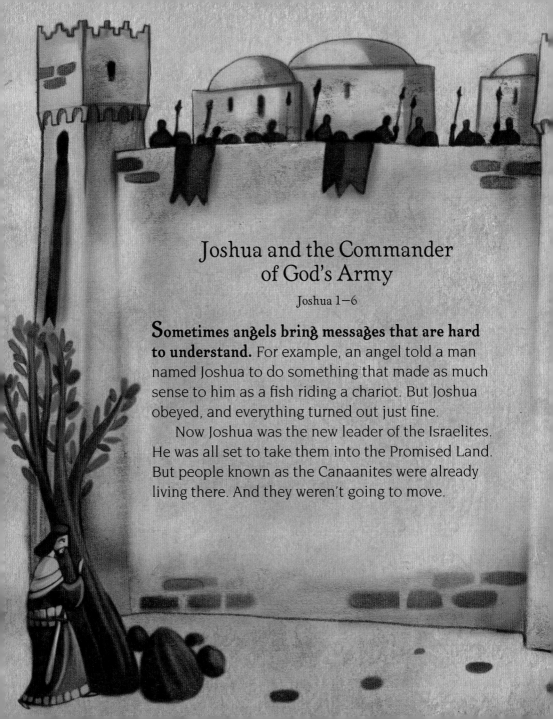

Joshua and the Commander
of God's Army

Joshua 1–6

Sometimes angels bring messages that are hard to understand. For example, an angel told a man named Joshua to do something that made as much sense to him as a fish riding a chariot. But Joshua obeyed, and everything turned out just fine.

Now Joshua was the new leader of the Israelites. He was all set to take them into the Promised Land. But people known as the Canaanites were already living there. And they weren't going to move.

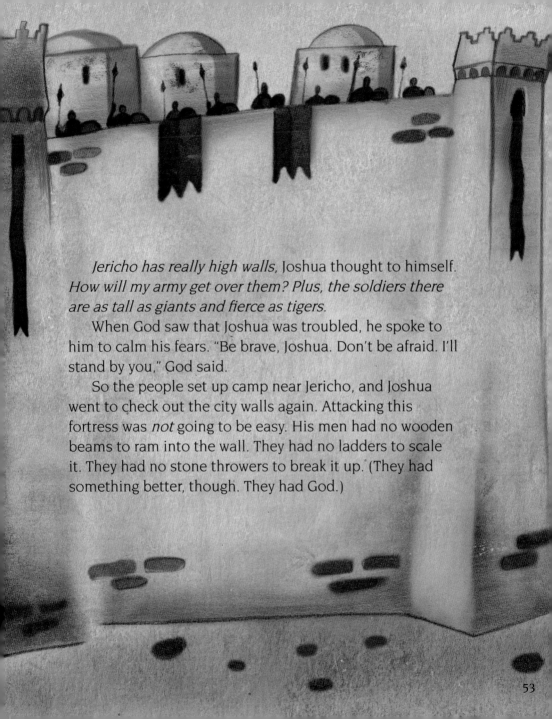

Jericho has really high walls, Joshua thought to himself. *How will my army get over them? Plus, the soldiers there are as tall as giants and fierce as tigers.*

When God saw that Joshua was troubled, he spoke to him to calm his fears. "Be brave, Joshua. Don't be afraid. I'll stand by you," God said.

So the people set up camp near Jericho, and Joshua went to check out the city walls again. Attacking this fortress was *not* going to be easy. His men had no wooden beams to ram into the wall. They had no ladders to scale it. They had no stone throwers to break it up. (They had something better, though. They had God.)

Suddenly, a tall warrior in full battle armor stood in front of Joshua. He had his sword raised. And he looked very scary. Joshua thought it might be one of the giant soldiers from Jericho.

"Are you for us, or against us?" Joshua asked bravely.

"Neither," the man said. "I am the Commander of the Army of the Heavenly Hosts. I'm here to fight the Lord's battle."

Joshua bowed his head low. "Did you bring any orders for me?" he asked.

"Take off your sandals," the angel said. "You're on holy ground."

This wasn't exactly what Joshua expected. But he wasn't about to question the Commander of the Heavenly Hosts. So off came his sandals.

After that, Joshua knelt while the angel told him how God was going to take Jericho. It made absolutely no sense. But if Joshua had learned one thing in his lifetime, he knew to obey God and trust in his way. So he got the details and returned to camp.

"Here's God's plan," Joshua told the people. "Starting tomorrow, you soldiers will walk around Jericho once—in silence. No talking, whistling, humming, nothing. Not a sound but marching feet.

"The priests will come next, blowing their rams' horns. And behind them, the other priests will carry the Ark of the Covenant. A rear guard will follow. Oh, and we'll do this for six days," Joshua said.

On the night before the seventh day, Joshua had more instructions. "Tomorrow, we're doing something different. Instead of once, we're circling the walls seven times," he said. "When we're finished, the priests will give one long, loud blast of their horns.

"Then I'll yell 'SHOUT!'" Joshua said. "And I want every man, woman, and child to scream their heads off. And don't stop until I tell you."

The next day everyone marched around the city six times—*stomp, stomp, stomp,* with the horns blasting, *ba-daaaaa-da, ba-daaaaa-da, ba-daaaaa-da.* The priest stopped, took a deep breath, and blew his horn. At the same time, Joshua hollered, "SHOUT! FOR THE LORD HAS GIVEN YOU THE CITY."

A great roar went up. And those huge walls came crumbling, tumbling down. Then Joshua and his men charged in, defeated their enemy, and took over the city. Because Joshua trusted God, he won a battle no one thought he would.

Gideon Asks for a Sign

Judges 6–7

God sometimes asks people to do things they're not too sure they can do. That's what happened to a man called Gideon. But God sent an angel to assure him he was definitely the man for the job.

Now at this time, the Israelites had sinned and turned away from God. So God allowed their enemies to conquer them. Things got so bad people hid in the hills and lived in caves. In their misery, they cried out, "Lord, please save us." And God heard them.

So one day, when their leader, Gideon, was gathering wheat, God sent an angel. The angel arrived quietly and sat under a nearby tree.

"God is with you, mighty warrior," the angel said, scaring Gideon out of his sandals.

"With me, sir?" Gideon asked. "If the Lord is with me, why are such awful things happening?"

The angel pretended he didn't hear Gideon. "I'm sending you to save your people," he said.

Gideon sighed. "With respect, sir, why me?" he asked. "My tribe is the weakest, and I am no hero. I think you need someone else."

"No, Gideon," the angel said. "God needs *you*. And don't worry. You *will* defeat your enemies."

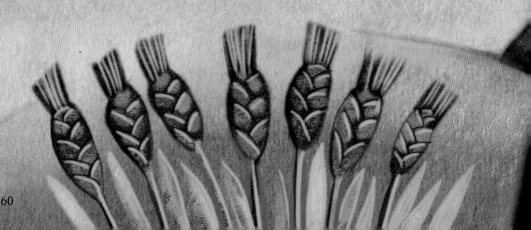

"Well," Gideon answered, "I'm thrilled you think I can take on this battle. But I'm a little worried. Why don't I go get some food as an offering? In the meantime, maybe you can come up with a sign? You know, something to prove that I'm *really* the one God wants."

When Gideon returned, the angel told him to place the plate of food on a rock. Then he touched it with the end of his staff. Gideon heard a *pop!* and a huge flame shot up. It burnt the food, the rock, and the ground below. "Okay," Gideon said to the angel. "I believe you." But when he looked, the angel had already gone.

So Gideon rounded up volunteers for his army. He told them God's angel had spoken to him. And he said the angel assured him they'd have victory.

But just before the fighting began, God said, "You have too many men." Then God explained. "I want the people to realize it's not you and your army who are saving them, but—me—the God who loves them. So tell any man who's afraid to go home." Gideon did and 22,000 men walked away.

But God still wasn't satisfied. So he showed Gideon how to cut his army even more until only 300 soldiers were left.

A nervous Gideon gave each fighter a horn, a lit torch, and a clay jar. Then he stationed them around a hill. The idea was to surprise the sleeping enemy soldiers.

"When I give the signal," Gideon said, "do what I do." A second later, Gideon shouted, "For the Lord and for Gideon!" He blew his trumpet and smashed his jar. His men did the same. And the enemy soldiers bolted upright. That's when Gideon and his men charged into the camp. As they did, God caused the enemy to get confused. So they turned and started fighting each other.

When the battle was over, God had given the victory to Gideon. Three hundred men had defeated thousands. After that, there was peace for forty years. And Gideon never had to bother an angel for a sign ever again.

A Long-Awaited Son

Judges 13:6—8

Angels don't have babies. But they are often sent to tell a woman a child is on the way.

That's just what happened to Mrs. Manoah. Now Mrs. Manoah was a godly person. She lived a holy life with her husband, Mr. Manoah. She had no sons or daughters. Still, she never gave up hope that she would have a child. So she prayed and prayed. And God had pity on her.

One day, when she was out in the field, she got a visit from an angel. He got right to the point.

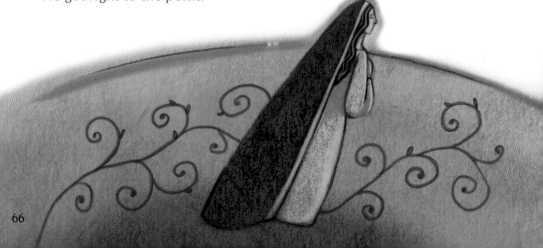

"I understand you couldn't have a baby before," he said. "But I am here to tell you you're pregnant right now. And soon you'll have a son."

Mrs. Manoah's jaw dropped. But she stood perfectly still. She didn't want to miss a word the angel said.

"Now, while you're pregnant," the angel continued, "I want you to take really good care of yourself. Don't drink wine. Eat lots of good food. And when your son is born, no strong drink for him either. He is to be dedicated to God. And here's the best part," the angel said. "God will use him to deliver his people from their enemies."

I better go tell my husband, Mrs. Manoah thought. So she left the angel and ran home.

"Sit down, dear," she said to Mr. Manoah when she arrived. "I just spoke with a stranger and I think he was an angel. He told me I'll have a son, who will grow up to be a holy man. He said God will bless him and make him a leader of our people. What do you think about that?"

Mr. Manoah sat quietly. He didn't know what to think. It bothered him that the angel hadn't brought the news to him first.

So that night he asked God to send the stranger again. "Lord," he prayed, "can you send this visitor back to us? I want to find out more about this son we are to have."

So the angel got word to return and went back—one more time—to Mrs. Manoah.

When she saw him, Mrs. Manoah rushed to get her husband. "He's here! He's here!" she said, dragging Mr. Manoah into the field.

"Sir," Mr. Manoah said, "are you the man who spoke to my wife?"

The angel nodded, "I am."

"I hear we are to have a son. Is there anything special he'll require? How should he be educated?" Mr. Manoah asked.

"Do everything I told the woman," the angel said.

Mr. Manoah sighed. It was plain to see the angel wanted to deal with his wife—not him. But at least he could show this heavenly visitor some hospitality. So he invited him to dinner.

"I'll stay a minute," the angel replied. "But I'm not really hungry. Why don't you give my share to the Lord as a thank you?"

So Mr. Manoah lit a fire and put the food on it. Then, suddenly, Mrs.Manoah tugged on her husband's sleeve and pointed. The angel was IN the fire. He was floating up to heaven on the flames. Mrs. Manoah grabbed her husband's hand and yanked him onto his knees. Both of them bowed their heads and began praising God.

A couple of minutes later, they looked up. The fire was out. The angel was gone. And they never saw him again.

"We're going to die. We've seen an angel, and we're going to die," Mr. Manoah cried out. He finally understood who the stranger was.

His wife put a hand on his shoulder. "Don't worry," she said. "Look, would God send an angel to tell us I'm pregnant if he were going to kill us? God loves us and has blessed us."

Mr. and Mrs. Manoah's son was born soon after. They named him Samson. And as the angel foretold, he saved God's people from their enemies.

Food for Elijah

1 Kings 18:16–39; 19:1–15

Angels do more than deliver messages. A holy man named Elijah found out they make great bread too.

It all started with a queen named Jezebel. She didn't believe in the real God. Instead, she worshipped a fake god called Baal. She built big temples to Baal and hired lots of priests. Sadly, this impressed some of God's people (the Israelites). So they began to worship Baal too.

God's friend, Elijah, wanted to prove Baal was a fake—a make-believe god. So he challenged Queen Jezebel's priests to a contest. "My God against your god," he said.

The day of the test arrived. The Baal priests put wood and their offerings on the altars. Then they called on their god to send down fire. Nothing happened. So they yelled, jumped up and down, and begged Baal to show his power. Still nothing.

"My turn," Elijah said.

"Almighty Lord," Elijah prayed. "Show everyone that you are the one true God. Send …"

ZAP! God didn't wait for Elijah to finish. A huge fire with orange-red flames licked up the offering, the wood, the rocks, the soil, and every last drop of water in the trench. "The Lord is God," the Israelites shouted. "Praise to the Lord," they yelled and dropped to their knees.

Now Queen Jezebel heard what happened. So she sent Elijah a message. "I swear by the gods I hold sacred," she wrote, "I will get you back for what you did, or my name isn't Jezebel."

"I better go and hide," Elijah said to himself.

So Elijah took off into the desert. "Lord," he prayed, "I'm a failure as a prophet. Why not just let me die under this tree?" He was very sad. To shut out his feelings, Elijah closed his eyes and fell asleep.

Now Elijah was actually a pretty good prophet. He was just having a really bad month. So God sent an angel to cheer him. The angel placed bread on some hot coals to heat. Then he set out the food and some cool water nearby.

"Elijah," the angel said gently, "time to get up and eat."
Elijah opened his eyes, saw the angel, and smelled the bread.
He ate a piece and he felt much better. Soon, though, he
nodded off again. The angel waited patiently and let Elijah
doze for a while. Then he woke Elijah one more time.

"Elijah," the angel said, "eat some more. It will give you
energy for your trip."

When Elijah finished, the angel was gone. So Elijah set out for the mountains. *No one will find me there,* he thought.

But God found him. "Aren't you supposed to be dealing with the false god Baal?" God asked.

"I ran away," Elijah answered. "Your people don't listen to me anymore. And Queen Jezebel has sent her men to kill me. That's why I'm here," he said boldly.

God listened to Elijah complain. Then he said, "Don't worry, Elijah. I'll protect you. You don't have to hide. In fact, I need you to go back right away. I want you to anoint two kings for me."

Elijah was relieved. With God on his side, he realized no one could harm him. He knew, too, that God's angels were always watching over him. That put a big smile on his face. So he left the mountains and went back to doing God's work.

King Hezekiah and One Awesome Warrior

2 Kings 18–19, 2 Chronicles 29–32

God has heavenly armies ready to do battle for him. But he sent only one angel to help his friend King Hezekiah.

Hezekiah became king when he was very young. The first thing he did when he put on his crown was to get rid of the false gods. Then he purified the temple so it was fit for worship. After that, he invited God's people, the Israelites, to return. The people knelt and prayed, played harps and lyres, and sang songs. Everyone was happy to be back in the house of the Lord.

While Hezekiah was busy making things right with God, his enemies, the Assyrians, were busy fighting with nearby nations. And Hezekiah knew it wouldn't be long until they would attack his people.

"Don't worry," God told Hezekiah. "I'll handle this. I'll protect you."

But Hezekiah didn't listen. *I'm not waiting until the enemy's at my front door,* he thought. *I'm going to stop them now.* So he joined forces with another king who was also battling the Assyrians.

But his plan didn't work. God was not pleased. Hezekiah was defeated big time. And this victory made the Assyrian king even bolder.

"I'm the greatest general, I'm number one," he bragged. "My army is unstoppable," he boasted. Then he got an idea: *The Israelites saw with their own eyes how I defeated Hezekiah in this last battle. So maybe I can just scare them into surrendering. It's worth a try.*

With that, the Assyrian king sent a message to the Israelites. "Men of Israel," the messenger shouted. "Lay down your weapons. We crushed your king, Hezekiah, before, and we'll crush him again. He says your God will defeat us. That's a lie. I tell the truth. Give up and live, or fight and die."

King Hezekiah heard about this and felt awful. He knew he should have let God deal with the Assyrians. So he sent for Isaiah, the holy man, to plead with God to forgive him. He also asked Isaiah to find out what God wanted him to do next.

While he waited for an answer, Hezekiah got a note from the Assyrian king that read: "Face it, you and your God are no match for us. Our army will surely overpower you." Hezekiah took the message to the temple. He spread the paper on the floor and knelt beside it.

"Lord," he said, "I deserved what I got. But look at what this king has written. He's making fun of you, Lord. Show him and every ruler near and far that you are the Almighty, the one and only powerful God."

God replied, and Isaiah delivered his answer to Hezekiah. "Here's what the Lord told me to tell you," Isaiah said.

"The Assyrian king has nothing to boast about. Yes, he won a lot of battles. But only because I allowed it. Now I will send him home in shame. As for his army," God said, "not one of his soldiers will put a foot inside your city. Wait and see."

"Thank you, God," Hezekiah said, "for forgiving me and for being so kind to me."

Nighttime came, and the Assyrian army was sleeping. So God sent his most powerful commander, the Angel of the Lord, to the battlefield. Nobody saw what happened. And nobody heard a thing. But in the morning, 185,000 Assyrians were dead.

Did God send a single angel to defeat a whole army on purpose? Was it to prove to the Assyrian king just how powerful he is?

The king didn't stick around to find out. He escaped and ran back to his hometown in disgrace. God had protected his people, just as he told Hezekiah he would. And he did it with one awesome angel.

Angels in the Throne Room

Isaiah 6:1—8

Angels take different forms when they appear. Some say they seem like ordinary people. Others say they could be mistaken for mighty warriors. But a man named Isaiah described the angels he saw as, well, very strange looking indeed.

Isaiah was in the temple praying when he first saw them. As he knelt quietly, he saw a vision of heaven. Suddenly, God was in front of him. He was sitting on a magnificent throne. And he was wearing a royal robe with a long flowing train.

Isaiah saw angels too. There were thousands of them. They flew above and around God worshiping him. They looked like men—except that each had six large wings. One set of wings covered their faces. Another set covered their bodies. The third they used for hovering in the air. They were on fire with love for God. And they glowed with a bright light.

As Isaiah stared at the creatures, he heard them sing: "Holy, holy, holy is the Lord God. Heaven and earth are filled with God's glory." The voices were so powerful that the temple walls trembled and the floors shook. Isaiah shook too.

Isaiah felt confused and frightened. *Why would God appear before a sinner like me?* he thought.

"Almighty Lord," he cried out. "I'm not worthy to look upon your face. I've lied. I've been mean to people. I haven't always kept your rules. And I'm ashamed of how I acted. I'm not fit to kneel before you."

Now God knew Isaiah wasn't perfect. Even so, God wanted him for an important job. He wanted Isaiah to be his prophet—to deliver messages to the Israelites for him. But God could see Isaiah felt guilty about something. So he sent an angel to tell Isaiah he was forgiven.

The angel touched Isaiah's lips. Then he whispered words of encouragement. "God knows you're sorry for disobeying him. And he forgives you," the angel said. "He has wiped away your sins. You don't have to feel like you're not good enough anymore. You're okay in God's sight now."

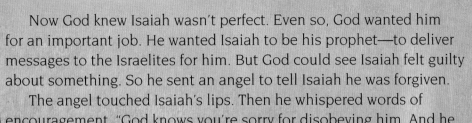

Isaiah's face brightened. He felt like a new man. He wasn't afraid anymore. He was finally ready for whatever God wanted. God saw this, so he made his request.

"I need someone to talk to the people on my behalf—to tell them what I want them to know," God said. "Is anyone willing to be my prophet?"

Isaiah waved his hand in the air. "Me, Lord," he shouted. "Send me. You have removed my sins, and I'm all set now. Please, Lord," Isaiah begged. "Send me."

So God made Isaiah his prophet. But he told him that the job wouldn't be easy.

"The people will be stubborn and won't listen," God said. But, like the angels he saw in the vision, Isaiah was on fire to serve God, no matter what. And for fifty years, that's just what he did.

The Stranger in the Fire

Daniel 3

God sometimes sends angels to get people out of a tight spot. In this story, an angel gets three faithful young men out of a hot spot.

It all began with the king of Babylon. His name was Nebuchadnezzar. Now, the king had fought God's people, the Israelites, and won. So he took a few of the smartest and most talented captives and put them to work in his royal court. He also changed their names to Shadrach, Meshach, and Abednego.

The three young men were fast learners and soon became the king's favorites. Still, they never forgot they were followers of the real God. So they prayed every day and kept God's rules.

But Nebuchadnezzar's false gods were beginning to bore him. So he built a huge new golden idol that was ninety feet high and nine feet wide. When it was finished, the king invited his subjects to celebrate.

"You are hereby ordered to come to a party in honor of my new golden idol. When the music begins," he said, "you are to bow low and worship. Those who don't obey will be thrown into the king's fiery furnace."

The day of the party came, and Nebuchadnezzar gave the signal. Everyone bowed. Everyone except three men. The king didn't notice. But some of his officials saw them and ran to tell him.

"Your Supremeness," the tattletales said, "Shadrach, Meshach, and Abednego say your god is false—just a statue. They refused to worship it."

King Nebuchadnezzar was furious. "Bring them to me!" he shouted.

"Yes, your majesty?" Shadrach said, when the three men stood in front of the king's throne. "You wanted us?"

"What I want, Shadrach," the king said, "is for you and your buddies to obey me. Now, in case you didn't understand the order—we'll try this again.

"When you hear the music, you are to turn, kneel, and worship my statue. If you won't, my men will tie you up and drop you into the fiery furnace like an egg in boiling water. Got that?"

"Sorry, but we can't," all three said in unison.

"We only worship the one, true God," said Shadrach.

"And if you try to harm us, our God will save us," said Meshach.

"And if he decides not to, that's okay. We'll still remain faithful to him because he loves us and we love him," said Abednego.

"That's it," Nebuchadnezzar yelled. "Throw them into the fire. Oh, and make it seven times hotter than usual. We'll just see if their God rescues them." The soldiers followed the king's orders. The crowd watched in horror.

A few minutes later, the king jumped up from his throne and started screaming. "Wait a minute! We threw three men into the fire, and now there are four," he screeched. "Is this some kind of a trick?"

There *were* four figures in the furnace. But it wasn't a trick. The fourth man was an angel. God sent him to stand in the fire and make sure the flames didn't harm Shadrach, Meshach, and Abednego.

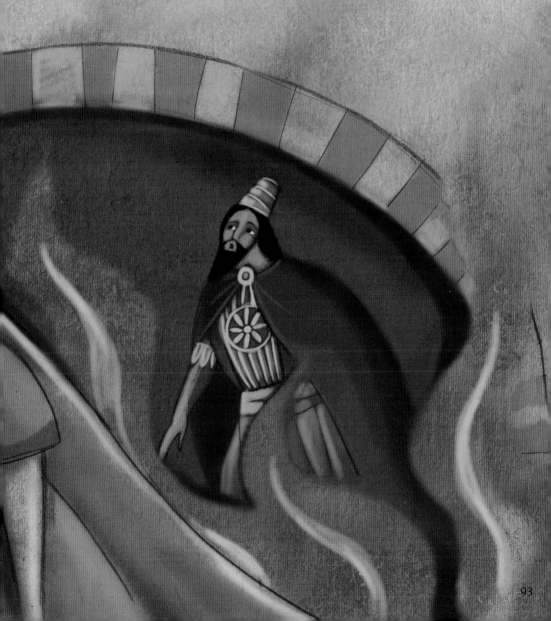

King Nebuchadnezzar looked confused. "Everyone in that furnace, come out now!" he shouted. And when he counted, one, two, three men stood in front of him—Shadrach, Meshach, and Abednego. They weren't hurt. They didn't even smell like smoke. They looked exactly like they had when they were thrown in.

The stranger in the fire, meanwhile, disappeared.

"Well," said the king, "I'm impressed. Your God actually *did* keep you safe." Then he spoke to the crowd.

"We've all witnessed what happened here. These men were willing to give up their lives rather than give up their God," he said. "God rewarded their faith and sent an angel to save them. And that was some rescue. No other god could have done that. So from now on," King Nebuchadnezzar said, "we will all respect the God of the Israelites … or else."

Lion Tamer

Daniel 6

Shadrach, Meshach, and Abednego had a close friend named Daniel. He lived at the court in Babylon too. Daniel had visits from angels on a few occasions. The most unforgettable was an angel who was an expert with cats.

After Nebuchadnezzar and his son ruled, a new king came on the scene. His name was Darius the Mede. He had heard good things about Daniel. So he let him continue working at the palace. And Daniel, as always, did a super job. Because of this, the king made Daniel the boss.

Now Daniel was also good at praying. Three times a day, every day, he knelt and worshiped the Lord.

But two of the governors who worked at the palace were jealous of Daniel. So they came up with a plan to get rid of him.

"Your Wonderfulness," the first governor said to the king. "Isn't it time for a decree to celebrate how awesome you are?"

"See here, Your Greatness," the second governor chimed in. "We've written one for you. It orders everyone to pray only to you, as you are our most excellent king. Those who disobey will be punished."

"Sounds good to me," the king said. So he put his "X" on the paper. The two governors grinned from ear to ear. Once signed, a law could not be changed.

Soon after, Daniel admitted to praying to the real God. When he did, the king had to obey his own law. "I'm sorry, Daniel," the king said. "But there's nothing I can do."

"Don't worry, Your Grace," Daniel shot back. "My God will rescue me." The king had Daniel thrown into the lions' den. When Daniel's eyes got used to the darkness, he looked around. There were lions everywhere. The first thing he did was to kneel and pray. He knew God would protect him. Still, he did feel a bit afraid.

Suddenly, a really big cat with pointy teeth noticed him and started to drool.

"Lord," Daniel prayed, "I don't mean to rush you. But help now would be greatly appreciated." At that, the lion crouched, roared, and got ready to pounce. Daniel closed his eyes.

When he opened them, he saw an angel. A bright light surrounded him and lit up the whole den. Daniel's eyes darted from the angel to the lions. Their mouths were shut.

"Thank you, God. Thank you a million times over," Daniel said. "And thank you, kind sir," he said as he turned toward the angel. But when he looked, the angel was gone. Daniel smiled. Then he picked out a comfortable rock and went to sleep.

The next morning, Daniel woke to hear King Darius shouting, "Daniel, Daniel, are you all right?"

"Yes, Your Highness," Daniel answered. "There's not even one scratch on me. God sent his best lion-tamer angel to shut the lions' mouths. It was amazing," Daniel said. "But then, God *is* amazing."

"Hurray for your God," the king said. Then he ordered the soldiers to remove the stone. When Daniel came out, the king gave him a big hug.

Back at the palace, the king praised Daniel's God for sending an angel to protect his friend from men—and beasts. Then he ordered the mean officials to be carted off to the lions' den themselves.

Afterward, he wrote a new law ordering everyone to pray to Daniel's God—the one and only true God. Daniel was so happy he went up to his room to pray.

Daniel's Message Gets Delayed

Daniel 10–12

When God sends an angel on a mission, he goes lickety-split. There is no dilly-dallying. But one time, a good angel got held up by a bad angel. So it took him twenty-one days to deliver God's news.

Daniel was an old man by now. And he had questions about the future of God's people. So he prayed hard every day for answers.

Nothing happened. *This is not like God,* Daniel thought. *The Lord is always quick to get back to me. I'll try again.* The next week, Daniel prayed longer and harder.

Still nothing. But Daniel trusted the Lord and kept on praying. Then, one afternoon while Daniel walked by the river, a magnificent-looking angel stood in front of him. He was dressed in white with a gold sash and his body shone like flashes of lightning.

Daniel gasped. Every hair on his body stood up. And when the angel spoke, Daniel's knees caved in and he fell to the ground.

A second later, he felt a hand lift him up.

"Don't be scared, Daniel," the angel said. "God loves you. He heard your prayers the minute they were out of your mouth. And he sent me with the answers."

Before Daniel could ask him—what took so long—the angel spoke again.

"Yes, Daniel, I know it has taken me ages to get here," the angel said. "And believe me, I tried to come sooner."

The angel took a deep breath. Then he explained why he was late.

"A fallen angel who calls himself 'Prince' was stirring up trouble in Persia," the angel said. "I was there trying to stop him when I got orders to leave. I started out, but that bad angel Prince blocked me. I was stuck for days. I finally had to call for help."

Daniel was surprised. "Help?" he said. "Who did you call?"

"Michael, one of the archangels," the angel replied. "He was there in an instant and dealt with Prince. And that freed me to make my way to you."

"Well, do you have any answers for me?" Daniel asked.

"I do," the angel said. Then he sat Daniel down and told him in great detail what would happen to the Israelites far into the future. It was a story of kings of the north and kings of the south, of fierce battles, the rescue of good people, and the fate of the bad.

"But, sir, please," Daniel said. "What will the final outcome be?"

The angel sighed.

"What I'm telling you now is top-secret," he said. "It's from God's very own Book of Truth. God is letting you have this information because you're his friend and because you never stopped praying. But I can't tell you everything," the angel said. "Just be assured things will become clear when the time is right. And God will definitely be there for his people."

Then, as silently as he had appeared, the angel left. Daniel whispered a prayer of thanks, then made his way home. When he got there, he wrote himself a note: "Reminder: When waiting for answers from God, be patient. The angels are very busy."

 God's good angels are in constant battle with Satan's bad angels. (Dan. 10:12, 20)

NEW TESTAMENT

———◆———

All angels are spirits who serve.
God sends them to serve those
who will receive salvation.

Hebrews 1:14

A Son for Zechariah

Luke 1:5–23

When an angel brought some news to a priest named Zechariah, the visit left him speechless.

Zechariah was in the temple when the angel appeared.

"Hello, Zechariah," the angel said. "Please, don't be afraid. I won't hurt you. I'm here to tell you something that will make you very happy. You're going to be a father. You're going to have a son. And God wants you to call him John."

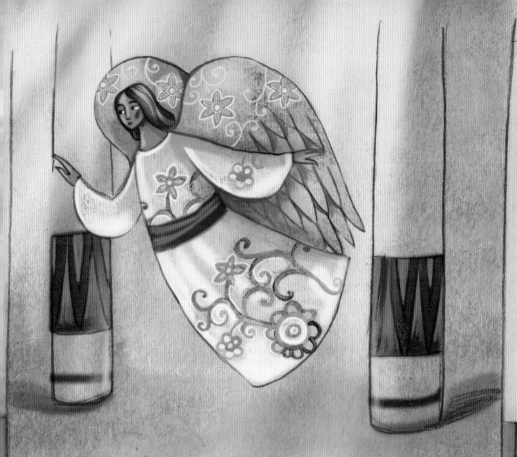

Zechariah took a step back. He was confused. He and his wife, Elizabeth, had prayed for a child all their lives. But they never had one. And now Elizabeth was way past the age of having babies.

The angel could see that Zechariah was puzzled. "Yes, Zechariah," the angel said. "You and your wife will soon be parents. And when the boy grows up, he'll do important work. He'll bring sinners back to God. And he'll prepare people for something amazing. God is sending his Son to earth, and your son will get everyone ready. Isn't that wonderful?"

"Well, it *would* be if it were true," Zechariah said. "But I don't know. Do you have the right couple? Are you sure about this?"

The angel looked at Zechariah and said, "I am Gabriel. I sit in God's presence all day. And I know that anything God wants to do is possible. Trust me."

"I'm trying to," Zechariah said. "But …"

"Okay," said Gabriel. "You don't believe me. I see that. So I'm shutting off your voice. From now on you won't be able to talk."

"But don't worry, Zechariah." Gabriel continued. "You'll be able to speak when your son is born." Then he disappeared.

Zechariah put his hand to his mouth. He tried to say something, but nothing happened. *Oh my goodness,* he thought. *It's really true. We're going to have a son.*

When Zechariah got home, he motioned for his wife to give him something to write on. "I saw an angel," he scribbled. "You're going to have a child." Elizabeth read the note, jumped up, and hugged Zechariah. Then she danced around the table and hugged him again. She had no doubts. She only had joy.

A few months later the baby was born. Relatives thought he would be called Zechariah after his father. But the proud dad had other ideas. He grabbed his writing tablet and jotted the name *John* on it.

As soon as he did, Zechariah's voice came back, just as the angel Gabriel said it would. "Thanks be to the Lord for blessing us with this son," Zechariah said. And everyone could hear him.

When the boy grew up, he was known as John the Baptist. And just as the angel Gabriel predicted, John taught many people about God and saved lots of sinners.

 Most angels don't give out their names. But in this story, Gabriel told Zechariah who he was and why God sent him.

A Surprise Visitor

Luke 1:26–38

Gabriel wasn't back in heaven long when he got another assignment. This time, God sent him to Elizabeth's cousin—a young Jewish girl named Mary.

Mary grew up in Nazareth, in Galilee. Like any other teenage girl in her village, her days were filled with chores. She baked bread, spun wool, and fed and cared for the animals. Yet she always took time to pray. So Mary grew very close to God. And God loved her very much.

When the time came for Mary to marry, her parents made the arrangements. They chose a kind man who worked as a carpenter. His name was Joseph. And like Mary, he prayed a lot too. When Mary's pledge to Joseph was settled, she returned home to prepare for her wedding.

That's when the angel Gabriel paid her a visit.

"Hello, Mary, blessed one," Gabriel said. "The Lord is with you."

Mary turned to face a stranger wearing a brilliant robe. She had never seen an angel before. But she was pretty sure she was seeing one now.

"Forgive me, sir," she said, falling to her knees. "I'm just a poor village girl. Why would you talk to me like that?"

"Mary please, don't be afraid," Gabriel said. "I was sent from God to give you a message. You're going to have a baby. He'll be a holy child. God wants you to call him Jesus."

Mary took a deep breath. "Sorry, sir," she answered. "I don't understand. How can I have a child? I just got engaged. I don't have a husband yet."

"Leave that to God," Gabriel said. "He will take care of it. He will send the Holy Spirit to you. And the child you'll have will be God's Son."

Mary loved God with all her heart. So she answered the angel without hesitating. "I am God's humble servant," she said. "I will do whatever he wants me to do."

"Amen," said Gabriel. Then he disappeared.

Telling Joseph about Jesus

Matthew 1:18–24

Angels usually appear to people when they are awake—but not always. God sent Mary's husband-to-be, Joseph, a message in a dream. It was about Mary's baby. And an angel delivered it.

Now Mary and Joseph were engaged. But they were not husband and wife. Mary lived with her parents. And Joseph remained in his home. So when Joseph heard that Mary was going to have a baby, he thought: *We're not married yet. How can I be a father?*

Joseph didn't know about the miracle God had performed. God hadn't told him yet.

I don't want to hurt Mary, Joseph thought to himself. But the right thing to do is to cancel the wedding.

After Joseph made up his mind, he was tired and fell asleep. When he did, he had a wonderful dream.

A magnificent-looking angel stood beside him. "I can see you're disappointed," the angel said. "But don't be. God has chosen Mary to be the mother of his Son. He loves her *that* much.

"And at this very minute," the angel said, "Mary is pregnant by the Holy Spirit. This is all part of God's plan. And in a few months, she will have a baby—the Messiah. God wants you to call him Jesus."

Joseph had read the Scriptures about this child. He was to be born of a young woman, the prophet Isaiah said. And he would be called Wonderful Counselor, Mighty God, and Prince of Peace. Could Mary *really* be that girl?

"So, Joseph, don't be afraid to marry Mary," the angel continued. "Go ahead with your wedding plans."

When Joseph woke up, he was relieved. The angel had lifted a great burden from his heart. So Joseph quickly knelt and prayed.

"Lord," he said, "Thank you for clearing things up for me. I am a happy man again. I know I'm unworthy for such a great honor. But with your help, I will love and take care of Mary and Jesus for as long as I live. Praise to your name forever."

Then Joseph hurried to tell Mary about his dream. And soon after, Joseph took the angel's advice. He made Mary his wife.

Voices Like Thunder

Luke 2:1–20

Angels have very good voices. Shepherds heard them the night Jesus was born. That's when God sent his very best choir to earth to sing for joy.

"We have to take a trip," Joseph said to Mary one day. Mary was surprised because it was almost time to have her baby. "The Romans want to know how many people they rule," Joseph said. "So we have to go to Bethlehem to be counted."

Mary packed for their journey. Then Joseph helped her onto their donkey.

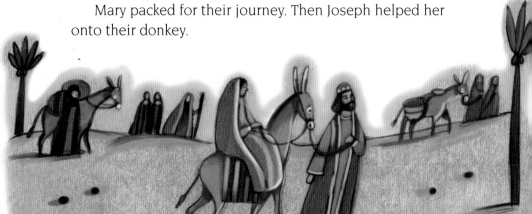

The road was rocky and rough. "Dearest Lord," Mary prayed, "please help us get there soon."

Days went by, and they finally reached the town. All Mary could think about was a soft bed and a good night's sleep. Then, suddenly, she felt the baby move.

"Joseph," Mary said. "It's time for the child to be born. We need to find a place to stay quickly."

Joseph knocked on one door, then another. No luck. The town was bursting with visitors. Every house was full. All the rooms were taken.

"Sir," Joseph said to one innkeeper, "my wife is having a baby—any minute now. Please," Joseph pleaded, "do you have any shelter at all?"

The innkeeper glanced at Joseph then at Mary. The sad look on her face moved him to help. "I have a barn out back," he said.

"Bless you," Mary said. Then Joseph hurried her to the stable.

Now, in the hills outside Bethlehem, shepherds looked after their sheep. Darkness had spread out and colored the hills black. And all was quiet. Then, suddenly—*FLASH*—a blaze of light lit up the sky. The shepherds ran to the cliff's edge to see what caused it.

"A creature from heaven!" someone shrieked.

"It's an angel!" another yelled.

"Lord, help us!" another cried.

"Don't be afraid. I won't hurt you. I'm here to give you a message," the angel said. "The Messiah is here! He was born a few hours ago in Bethlehem. You'll find him in a barn behind an inn. He's wrapped in a blanket. And he's sleeping in a manger."

While the shepherds listened, hundreds of angels lit up the sky. "Glory to God in the highest," the angels sang in voices louder than thunder. "And peace on earth to all good men."

Then, suddenly, the night swallowed up the angels. And it was dark again.

"You heard what the angels said," shouted one shepherd. "Let's go and find this child." So the shepherds ran down the hill and into the town.

When they got there, the shepherds searched for
the child. Finally, one innkeeper pointed to his stable.
"Look for yourself," he said. So they did. And there he
was—lying in the soft hay.

"Angels—we saw angels!" one shepherd shouted at
Mary and Joseph. The shepherd repeated all the angel
had said. Everyone who heard the story was amazed.

"His name is Jesus," Mary told them.

Meanwhile, the angels were back in heaven looking
on. The shepherds couldn't hear them, but they were
still singing.

The Bible says that one angel's voice was like "the sound of a large crowd." So you can imagine what hundreds of angels sounded like.

Daniel 10:6

137

Warning Wise Men

Matthew 2:1–12

God kept the angels pretty busy around the time Jesus was born. **He sent angels with announcements and angels with warnings.** One of those warnings uncovered the secret plans of an evil ruler.

The man's name was Herod. He called himself "The King of the Jews." And he called himself "Great." But he was really just a bully who was mean to everyone.

One day, visitors came into Herod's city. They were wise men who studied the stars. They had seen a big, bright star and knew it meant an important king was about to be born. So they decided to find him and bring gifts.

When Herod's spies heard the wise men talking, they rushed to tell His Highness the news.

Herod listened. Then he shouted, "A king? I am the king! I am HEROD THE GREAT!" Then he stomped his foot and called for the wise men.

When they arrived, sneaky Herod turned on the charm. "Kind sirs," he said sweetly, "why have you come so far? Please sit and eat." So the men sat.

"We're looking for the new king," the first wise man said, grabbing some cheese.

"Yes, we saw his star in the East," the second wise man said, reaching for grapes.

"We've brought him presents," said the third wise man, tossing some nuts into his mouth.

Suddenly, Herod had an idea. "How about when you find this king, you tell me? Then I can go visit him myself," he asked. Of course, he was lying. "I'll pay you," Herod added.

"Sounds like a plan," the men answered.

The next day, the wise men continued on their journey. The star led them to a small house in Bethlehem. And they went inside.

"There he is! Look!" the first wise man shouted. A happy toddler was sitting and playing. He smiled at the men.

"His name is Jesus," Mary told them. The wise men opened their bags and pulled out their gifts. "For the new king," they said.

All too soon the men had to leave. They traveled until it got dark. Then they stopped for the night. "We can head to Herod's in the morning," they all agreed.

During the night, God sent a message to the men. An angel told them Herod wanted to hurt Jesus. He told them not to go anywhere near Herod's palace. He told them to go home another way.

At sunrise, the first wise man bolted upright and woke the others. "We can't go to Herod's," he said. "He wants to kill Jesus. An angel told me so."

"An angel told us as well," the other two wise men reported.

So they packed their bags, and they slipped out of town. Herod had tried to trick the wise men. But thanks to the angel, *they* tricked Herod instead.

The name "angel" means "messenger." That describes a lot of the work these beings do.

Jesus, the Children, and the Angels

Mark 10:13–16; Matthew 18:10

Jesus traveled to many cities and towns to talk about his Father. It was hard work. Everywhere he went crowds of people came to hear him. Many mothers brought their children so Jesus could bless them.

The children were excited to meet Jesus.

"I think I see him," a girl with wavy hair said to her brother.

"Is he the man with all the people around him?" the brother asked.

"Yes," the girl answered. "Mommy said he is God's Son and he's going to tell us all about heaven," she said, "Come on, let's run ahead."

It happens that on this particular day, Jesus had done even more preaching, teaching, and healing than usual. And he was really tired. So when his disciples saw the long line of children and mothers, they held their hands up and said, "Stop!"

"Jesus can't see anyone else today," one disciple said.

"Yes, especially children," another disciple said. "They're too noisy. They're covered with dirt. They'll climb all over him. What he needs now is rest."

Jesus overheard what the disciples were telling the mothers, and he scolded them. "Let those children through. Don't treat them like they don't matter. Because they do," Jesus said. "The kingdom of heaven belongs to these children and those who are like them. In fact, they are so important that God has appointed an angel for each one and that angel can speak to my Father anytime on their behalf."

"Take a good look at them," Jesus continued. "Because anyone who wants to be part of my kingdom has to accept me and be as excited to see me as these children are. So let them pass."

After that, Jesus gathered all the children around. He hugged them. He blessed them. And he told them all about his Father in heaven.

Meanwhile, somewhere nearby, the angels celebrated.

No specific stories feature guardian angels in the Bible. But King David wrote, "The Lord will command his angels to take good care of you. They will lift you up in their hands. Then you won't trip over a stone".

(Psalm 91:11—12)

Giving Strength to Jesus

John 18:1–12 ; Luke 22:39–48; Matthew 26:36–56

Jesus came to earth on a mission. He came to take the punishment for all the wrong things people did or would do. He came to wipe away everyone's sins. He came to give people a chance to live with him forever in heaven.

But for this to happen, he had to die on a cross. And when Jesus thought about that, all the strength drained out of his body. He needed an angel to comfort him.

Now it was nighttime, a few hours before Jesus was arrested. He had just finished eating a final meal with his friends. And, afterward, he felt troubled and sad.

Jesus needed to talk to his Father. So he took some of his disciples and went to a quiet olive garden. "Keep watch and pray with me," Jesus told his friends. "I'll go on a little further."

"Yes, Jesus. We will," they all answered.

Jesus came to a clearing and knelt on the ground. He thought again about what would happen to him. He would have to carry a big, heavy cross. The soldiers would hang him on it until he died. People watching would make fun of him. And even his best friends would run and hide. This filled his heart with sorrow and made his body weak.

Still, Jesus knew this was part of God's plan. And he loved people so much, he was willing to accept it. But it was terrifying. So he had to ask, "Father, I know what I have to do. But is there another way to save sinners? Before you answer," he added quickly, "I'm here to do what you want, not what's better for me."

Jesus waited. But all he heard was silence.

Jesus realized then he would have to suffer for everyone's sins by himself. There was no one else who could do it. There was no other way.

And God had to let him.

But God saw that Jesus was overwhelmed. So he sent one of his most powerful angels to Jesus' side.

When the angel arrived, Jesus felt strengthened. He knew God had sent this angel, not to take away the suffering, but to give him the power to withstand it.

The angel looked at Jesus one more time, then he turned to leave. Jesus knew then it was time to go. So he got up and went back to his friends. When he did, his body wasn't weak anymore, and his mind was made up. He was ready to give his life for the world.

Suddenly, a crowd of Jewish officials and soldiers surrounded Jesus. Sadly, Judas, one of Jesus' own friends, led the way. Judas greeted Jesus with a kiss. But Jesus knew the crowd had come to arrest him. So he let them.

The angels watched as the mob led Jesus away. Since God didn't summon them to rescue him, the angels could only do one thing—stare at Jesus in silence through sorrowful eyes.

Delivering the Best Message Ever

Matthew 27:57–65; Matthew 28:1–10; Luke 24; John 20:1–18

Jesus suffered and died for everyone's sins. That might seem like the end of the story. But it was really just the beginning.

After Jesus was taken down from the cross, his friends buried him in a rock cave. Then some men rolled a big stone in front of it. But Jesus' enemies wanted to make sure no one could break into the tomb. So they went to the Roman official, Pilate.

"You heard what those Jesus followers claim," the chief priest said. "Their 'Savior' will rise from the dead. I wouldn't be surprised if they steal his body to make this whole business look real. Can't you do something?" he asked.

"You might be right," Pilate said. Then
he called for his guards to put a seal on
the rock, and have soldiers stand watch.

Three days later, a miracle happened. Jesus rose from the dead. So God sent an angel to tell his friends.

But Jesus' friends were hiding. They were afraid the people who had killed Jesus would come after them. However, two of Jesus' friends decided to be brave and visit the grave. Their names were Mary and Mary.

As Mary and Mary walked along, they heard a loud noise. The angel God had sent was busy rolling away the tomb's big stone. Then he sat on it ready to announce the happiest, best, most jump-up-and-down-and-sing-hallelujah news that ever made its way from heaven to earth.

The women stared at the angel in wonder. The soldiers shook with fear and passed out.

"Kind women, don't be afraid," the angel said. "I know why you're here. You're looking for Jesus. I have some wonderful news for you: Jesus is risen just like he said he would."

The two women were so surprised they couldn't move.

"Please come inside and see for yourself," the angel said. "Then go quickly and tell the others. Give them this message: Jesus is alive. And he'll meet up with everyone soon."

The women walked into the cave slowly. It was empty. They looked around, but Jesus was not there. The only thing they saw was the cloth he had been buried in.

Mary and Mary turned to leave. By this time, the angel was gone.

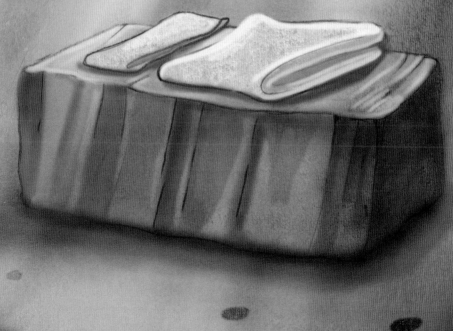

The two women ran down the road. "Jesus is alive!" they shouted. Suddenly, they bumped into a stranger.

"It's me—Jesus," he said. Mary and Mary were amazed.

"It's okay," Jesus said. "It really IS me. But before I do anything else, I must first go see my Father in heaven. So tell everyone I'll meet them in Galilee."

Mary and Mary hurried back and shared the good news.

Meanwhile, the angel who had delivered the best
message ever watched as Jesus ascended to his Father.

Watching Jesus Go Home

Acts 1:3–11; Mark 16:14–20; Revelation 5:11, 12

Angels are a part of Jesus' story from beginning to end.
And when Jesus finished his work on earth, angels looked on
as he returned to heaven.

After Jesus rose from the dead, he spent forty days visiting
with his friends, the disciples. Soon, though, it was time for
Jesus to go back home. So he took some of the men and went
to a high mountain.

"Friends," Jesus said tenderly, "I am leaving you now. But you will not be alone. I'm sending you the Holy Spirit—the Helper. When he comes, you will understand everything I taught you. Then it will be your job to spread this Good News everywhere.

"The Holy Spirit will give you the power to do wonderful things in my name," Jesus said. "Heal the sick, and bring people back to God. And not just here, but in Jerusalem, Judea, and in every single part of the world."

The disciples stood there listening. Then, suddenly, right in front of them, Jesus rose up into a big cloud and disappeared.

"Where did he go?" someone yelled. "Can anyone see him?"

All eyes were looking up. Everyone was straining to see if he could catch one last glimpse of Jesus, when a voice said, "My good men of Galilee, why are you staring at the sky?"

When the disciples turned their heads, they saw two angels dressed in long white robes.

"If you're looking for Jesus," one angel said, "he's gone back to heaven."

"And by now," the other angel said, "he's sitting at the right hand of the Father."

"But Jesus will come back again one day," the first angel said. "And he'll return to earth just as you've seen him go."

None of the disciples said a word. Nobody moved.

"Okay," the first angel continued, "you men have work to do. It's up to you to spread the Good News."

With that, the angels disappeared. And Jesus' friends walked back to Jerusalem to wait for the Holy Spirit.

Meanwhile, back in heaven, the two angels joined others praising and worshiping Jesus.

 The angels don't know when Jesus will return. But they know he will. And when he does come back to earth, all his angels will come with him.

Philip Listens and Obeys

Acts 8:26—40

Angels don't call to let people know they plan to visit. And they don't stick around to do a lot of explaining. So a person has to listen, trust, and do what the angel says—even if he doesn't quite understand.

The disciple Philip trusted God. And one day, when he received some strange instructions, he got a chance to prove it.

This happened in a place called Samaria. Philip was teaching the Good News to people who had never heard of Jesus. And he wanted to stay there. But God had other plans in mind.

One day, an angel appeared to Philip. Philip stood and listened. "I have a message for you from God," the angel said. "You must leave here at once. Go south, down the road that leads from Jerusalem to Gaza. You're to be there at noon."

Philip wondered: *Why would God want me to leave Samaria now, especially when I'm bringing so many people to Jesus?* Then another thought erased all the others. *If God wants me on the desert road at noon, he must have a reason.*

Other questions raced through Philip's mind. But all he said to the angel was "I'll grab a few things and go." The angel nodded. Then he disappeared.

When Philip arrived, he saw a fancy chariot in the middle of the desert road. A well-dressed man was sitting inside.

Philip heard a whisper telling him to go closer.

He did and got a big surprise. The official was studying God's Word.

"Good afternoon to you, sir," Philip said. "I am Philip, a follower of Jesus. Tell me, are those Scriptures you're reading?"

"I am the chief treasurer for Queen Candace of Ethiopia," the man replied. "And yes, I'm reading the book of Isaiah. I want to learn more about God."

"Isaiah?" Philip said. "That's my favorite. Do you understand it?"

"Well, I'm trying to," the official said. "But it's difficult. Could you spare some time to help me?"

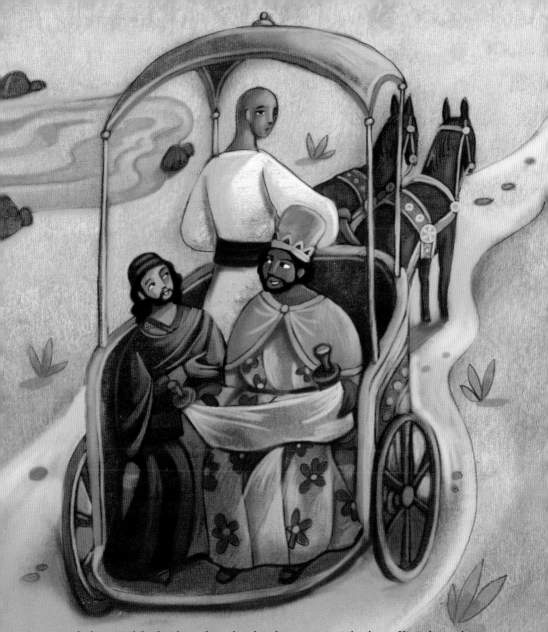

Philip nodded. Then he climbed up, sat with the official, and explained God's Word slowly. When Philip finished, the official's face was glowing. His heart was happy too.

Just then the driver asked a question. "Your Excellence?" he said. "We're coming to a stream. Can I stop and let the horses drink?"

"Good idea," the official said. Then he hopped off the chariot and ran to the water. "Baptize me, Philip," he said excitedly. "I believe in Jesus. I want him as my Savior."

"The Lord be praised," Philip said under his breath. Then he baptized the official. When the man returned home, he taught what he learned to others. Then they taught their friends too.

As a result, the Good News spread not only in Samaria where Philip started out, but also in Ethiopia where the official lived. Thousands more believed in Jesus because Philip trusted God and followed the angel's instructions.

Breaking Out of Jail

Acts 5:12–41

Angels can do some pretty neat things—like opening locked doors without a key. This came in handy when friends of Jesus got into trouble with a mean high priest and his friends.

The high priest didn't like Peter and John. They drew crowds whenever they taught in the temple. This made the high priest jealous.

"They keep talking about this Jesus," one of the high priest's friends reported.

"Well, I have a cure for that," the high priest replied. "Stick these two in the public jail for a couple of nights. Then we'll see if they still feel like spreading their 'Good News.'"

So they locked Peter and John up and posted guards outside their cell.

Late that night, an angel came and opened the prison door. Peter and John followed him past the sleeping soldiers into the street.

"I have a message for you," the angel told them. "God wants you to go back to the temple and keep telling people about Jesus."

Peter and John looked at each other then at the angel. But he was gone. "Well," Peter said. "I guess we'd better get back to work." So they did.

In the morning, the priests sent guards to get Peter and John.

"I went to their cell," the captain said when he returned empty-handed. "It was locked, and my men were on duty. But no one was inside."

"What do you mean, no one was inside?" the high priest screamed.

"Sorry, sir," the captain said slowly. "The men … we put … in jail … last night … are not there now."

The priests all started talking at the same time, asking the same question: How in the world did these men get out of jail?

Just then, a soldier barged into the room. "Your Eminence, the men in question are actually here," he said. "They've been in the temple since daybreak."

"Well, don't just stand there," the high priest yelled. "Bring them to us. NOW!"

When the guards led Peter and John in, the high priest walked up to them and shouted: "Didn't we tell you to *stop* talking about Jesus?"

"Yes, you did," Peter answered. "But God wants us to keep talking about Jesus. And what God wants is far more important than what any man wants. Don't you agree?"

The high priest's face turned red. The rest of the priests shouted and shook their fists.

Just then, a teacher of the law raised his hand and called for silence. "Look," he said. "We've seen dozens of groups like this. They come and they go. And these Jesus followers will, too, if they're like the others.

"But, if these men really *are* speaking for the true God, and Jesus really *is* who they say he is, then nothing we do will stop them. And God will certainly not be happy with us if we stand in their way," he said.

When the teacher of the law finished speaking, the priests took a vote. They decided to punish the disciples, but then, let them go.

184

So Peter and John left. And the next morning, right on schedule, they were back in the temple doing what the angel told them to do. They were teaching people about Jesus.

Jesus Is for Everybody

Acts 10

Jesus gave his message to God's people, the Jews, first. So the Jews thought that God meant his word for them only. But God arranged for Jesus' friend, Peter, to meet a man named Cornelius who would help change all that.

Cornelius was an officer in the Roman army. He was a Gentile—which is what everyone called a person who was not a Jew. But Cornelius behaved as though he were a Jew. He didn't worship idols. He gave money to the poor. And he prayed regularly asking God to guide him and his family in the right way to live.

God noticed and sent an angel to give him this message.
"Cornelius," the angel said, "God has sent me with an
answer to your prayers. Here's what he wants you to do.
Send servants to the house of Simon, the tanner," the angel
said. "Tell them to ask Peter, the Jew, to come back here.
Then listen to what Peter will tell you."

Cornelius was puzzled. But he called for his servants anyway.
"I don't know who this Peter is," he told them. "But God wants me
to meet him. So you'd better try to bring him here."

Now something puzzling was going on at Simon's house too. Peter was resting before lunch. And he was having a very strange dream about food. In it, a voice told him to pick a meal from food that Gentiles eat, but Jews didn't.

Peter was shocked. "I can't" he said. "God doesn't want me to."

"No, Peter," the voice continued. "What God wants is for you to listen. He is telling you that it's okay."

Peter woke up. *God is trying to tell me something through this dream,* he thought. *I just have to figure out what it is.*

Just then, Cornelius' men arrived. They told Peter about the angel. Then they asked Peter and his friends to return with them.

A large group of Gentiles was waiting for Peter at Cornelius' house. They had all come to hear what he had to say. But there was one problem. Peter had always thought he should not preach to Gentiles— just as he thought he should not eat certain foods. But he realized now that was not what God wanted.

That's why God sent him the dream. And that's why God brought him to Cornelius' house. God was telling Peter he wanted everyone to be saved—Jews and Gentiles.

"Friends," Peter said, "God led me to you today for a reason. He wants me to tell you about his Son."

"If that's so," Cornelius said, "then, tell us, Peter. We're listening." So Peter stood there all night, talking about Jesus. When he was finished, God's Spirit came down and filled the hearts of every man, woman, and child there. They all believed. And they all raised their voices in thanksgiving.

Now, angels who were close by stopped when they heard the voices. Praise was coming from every corner of Cornelius' house. They were even happier when they realized where the prayers were coming from: the mouths of both Jews AND Gentiles.

Getting Peter Out of Prison—Again

Acts 12:1—24

Poor Peter. Every time he turned around, some mean official was throwing him in jail. Good thing God's angels are experts when it comes to rescues.

This time, it was wicked King Herod who decided to arrest him. King Herod would likely have killed Peter right away, but the people were celebrating a special holy day. So the king ordered his jailers to hold Peter in prison until it was over.

As the guards led Peter away, Herod rose to his feet. "Stop!" he yelled. "Didn't this man break out of jail before?" he asked the captain. "Do any of you remember that?"

"No, Your Highness," the captain replied. "But if Your Excellency wishes, I can find out."

"Never mind!" Herod screamed. "I *know* this is the man. But he won't get away this time. I want sixteen men watching this prisoner's every move. I want one soldier handcuffed to him on the right and one on the left," the king ordered. "If he so much as puts his pinky out of his cell, I'll hold you all responsible."

When the news spread that Peter was in prison, his friends were on their knees day and night asking God for a miracle.

God heard them and sent his best get-out-of-jail angel to handle the matter.

The angel slipped into Peter's cell and shook him. "Peter, wake up," he said. Peter rubbed his eyes and squinted. *I must be dreaming,* he thought. But when he looked again, the angel was still there.

"Hurry, we have to leave," the angel said. As Peter stared at the angel, the chains cracked and dropped to the floor. Peter and the angel walked out of the locked cell and past a group of guard stations. Finally, the angel led Peter to the city gate. *CLANK!* It swung open, and they stepped out.

"I see now that this is no dream," Peter said to himself. "God has rescued me yet again. It's a miracle." Then Peter turned to the angel to thank him. But he was gone.

Peter hurried to a friend's house nearby. "Hello?" he said, as he stood at the entrance.

Rhoda, the servant girl, heard Peter's voice. But she was so excited that she left him outside while she ran to tell the others.

"Peter's at the door! Peter's at the door!" she shouted.

No one believed her. "It can't be Peter. He's in jail," someone called to her.

KNOCK, KNOCK, KNOCK.

This time, the others heard the knocking. When they opened the door, they couldn't believe their eyes. "Praise the Lord, it IS Peter!" everyone shouted. Then they pulled him in and hugged him.

"Please, friends," Peter said. "Just listen." Then he told them every detail—how he was falsely accused. How Herod had him thrown in jail. How he was handcuffed and had more than a dozen men guarding him. And how God's angel rescued him.

Everyone was amazed.

"I can't stay long. They'll be looking for me," Peter said. "But make sure all of Jesus' friends who prayed for me hear what happened."

In the morning at Herod's palace, the king was jumping up and down in a rage. "You can't find him?" he yelled. "You mean you let the prisoner escape again? Well, you better say goodbye to your heads," he screamed. Then he ordered the prison guards to be taken away.

A little while later, Herod was meeting with some officials. They praised him and called him a "god." Herod beamed and accepted their praise. Big mistake. Glory like that should only ever go to the one true God.

When God saw this, he sent down another angel. But this angel didn't bring good news. And he didn't unlock any prison cells. This angel delivered God's judgment with a disease that did away with King Herod for good.

Paul Survives a Shipwreck

Acts 27

Jesus' friend Paul traveled everywhere teaching people the Good News. Still, many city officials thought he was a troublemaker. So they shipped him off to Rome with a gang of convicts. But his trust in God and news from an angel kept him afloat.

The weather was really stormy when the prisoners' ship was ready to leave port. "Captain," Paul said, "If we go now, we could lose everything— the cargo, the ship, and even our lives. I think we should wait a while."

Paul's guard, an officer named Julius, spoke up. "Look, Paul, the captain is in charge here. So if he says we go, we go. Period."

Paul shook his head and went to his cabin.

A few hours later, the winds picked up. Stinging rain came down hard and fast. Like giant hands, big waves scooped the ship up and—SMACK!—dropped it down again.

The crew tied down the cargo and yanked up the lifeboats. Then they closed their eyes and held on. Only one man wasn't afraid. Paul knew God was in control. So he slept right through the worst of the rough weather.

As Paul lay dreaming, God sent an angel.

"Hello, Paul," the angel said. "God has sent me to tell you that everyone on board will get to Rome safely. Unfortunately, the ship will ram into some rocks and sink," the angel said. "But there's an island with friendly natives close by. You and the crew can stay there through the winter. That's it. God speed, Paul," the angel said, and he disappeared.

Morning came, and Paul asked his guard if he could speak to the crew.

"I've got some good news," Paul said. "Last night, God sent an angel to tell me everything will be okay. He said no one is going to drown. We'll all be saved."

Everyone, even Julius, let out a great big, "Hurray!"

Time passed, and the captain spied a safe inlet. He didn't realize it was a huge sandbar. By the time he figured it out, the ship was stuck. In a few hours, waves pounded it to bits.

"Kill the prisoners," one of the guards yelled. He didn't want Paul and the others to escape.

"Hold on!" shouted Julius. "I give the commands around here, and nobody is killing anybody. Every man who can swim, head to that island. The rest of you, hang on to some wreckage from the boat and make your way there."

So they swam and they floated to shore, and everyone survived.

A few months later, a passing ship took Paul and the others to Rome. All the passengers arrived safe and sound. But Paul always knew they would make it. The angel told him so.

A Better Place Filled with Angels

Revelation 1—22

When Jesus comes back, everything will be changed. The whole world will be better. Jesus gave his friend, John, a peek at that happy time. And John saw lots and lots of angels.

"Jesus was standing right next to me," John says. "But he didn't look like the Jesus I knew. His eyes were like black fiery coals. His face shone like the rays of a hundred suns. His voice was different too. When he spoke, it sounded like rushing waterfalls.

"Lord, is that really you?" John asked.

"Yes, John, it's me," Jesus answered. "Don't be afraid. I'm going to show you what will happen when I return. And I want you to write everything down. This way, my friends will have something to look forward to while they wait for me."

A second later, John found himself in a big, beautiful room. It was like the inside of a king's palace. Jesus was sitting on a high throne. He had a gold crown on his head, and there were angels everywhere. Some of the angels were singing beautiful worship songs. Others were playing musical instruments. And others were standing at attention as honor guards.

Suddenly, John heard a loud, clanging noise. That's when he saw a huge warrior angel drag the devil on a chain. The angel opened up a deep, dark pit and with one yank, threw Satan up and over and in. Then he sealed up the pit.

"That's the end of that misery for good and forever," the angel said.

Then John felt someone take his hand. A golden-haired angel led him to a high mountaintop. He stood there as a gigantic city, sparkling and gleaming, floated down in front of them. It was heaven. John's eyes widened at the sight of it.

The angel brought him closer, and he saw twelve gates made out of pearl. An angel stood in front of each, smiling. John saw shiny streets made of gold. There was no sun, because God's glory lit up everything.

Suddenly, from the throne room, Jesus spoke. "I'm making everything new again. From now on, there will be no pain, sickness, or death. I am getting rid of sadness and tears. No one will be alone or afraid because I will be with you," Jesus said.

"On the day that I return," Jesus said, "you'll hear the sound of an archangel's voice and the music of the trumpet of God. You'll see my angels too. They will gather believers from all over the world to join me. And from then on, you will always be with me. That's what will happen when I come again."

John took a deep breath and found himself back in his cell. Jesus was gone, but the angel was still there. So John fell on his knees.

"Please get up," the angel said quickly. "I'm just the messenger. Jesus is the one you should worship, not me. But John, listen to me. While everything is fresh in your mind, write about it," the angel said. Then he disappeared.

Later, John wrote down everything he had seen in a book called Revelation. He was careful to make sure he explained the wonderful new world Jesus is preparing for everyone who loves him.

When John got to the end, he finished with a short prayer. "Come soon, my Lord, Jesus. Your people are waiting."

And somewhere close by, the angel who visited John whispered,

"Let it be so."